For Bethan, Lucia, and Tilly

First U.S. edition 2013

Library of Congress Catalog Card Number 2012942675
ISBN 978-0-7636-6486-2

12 13 14 15 16 17 TLF 10 9 8 7 6 5 4 3 2 1

Printed in Dongguan, Guangdong, China

This book was typeset in Garamond.
The illustrations were done in watercolor and ink on paper.

TEMPLAR BOOKS

an imprint of Candlewick Press
99 Dover Street
Somerville, Massachusetts 02144

www.candlewick.com

Thomas Docherty

Wash-a-Bye BEAR

templar books
an imprint of Candlewick Press

"I love you, Bear," said Flora one morning.
"But Mommy says you are smelly and full of stains
and you need a wash."

"So you're going in the washing machine with all the dirty socks," she told him.

"Don't worry, Bear. I'm going to be right here
waiting for you.

Be brave, Bear!"

Wash away soggy breakfast smears.

Wash away melted ice-cream tears.

Wash away memories of the beach—

birthday cake and sticky sweets.

Wash away spatters of winter showers.

Wash away mud and rain-soaked hours.

Wash away scrapes from climbing trees—

hide-and-seek in fallen leaves.

Wash away glittery glue from clothes.

Wash away paint from paws and nose.

Wash away furious marker scribbles—

splats and spots and drips and dribbles.

And stop!

Poor, brave, dizzy Bear.

Clean, fluffy, wash-a-bye Bear.

"But now you don't look like Bear.

You don't smell like Bear.

You don't taste like Bear . . .

and you don't feel like Bear," said Flora sadly.

"Come on, Bear.
I know what
to do."

Back through all our teatime fun,

every smear and every crumb.

Back through noisy backyard games—
slippery slides and grassy stains.

Back through making things together, me and you forever and ever.

And stop!

"Now you're my Bear again," said Flora.

"But Mommy says now *I'm* all smelly and full of stains,
so I need a wash, too."

"Mommy," said Flora after her bath, "do you think Bear will still love me now that *I'm* all washed and clean?"

"Yes," said Mommy, "and he always will."

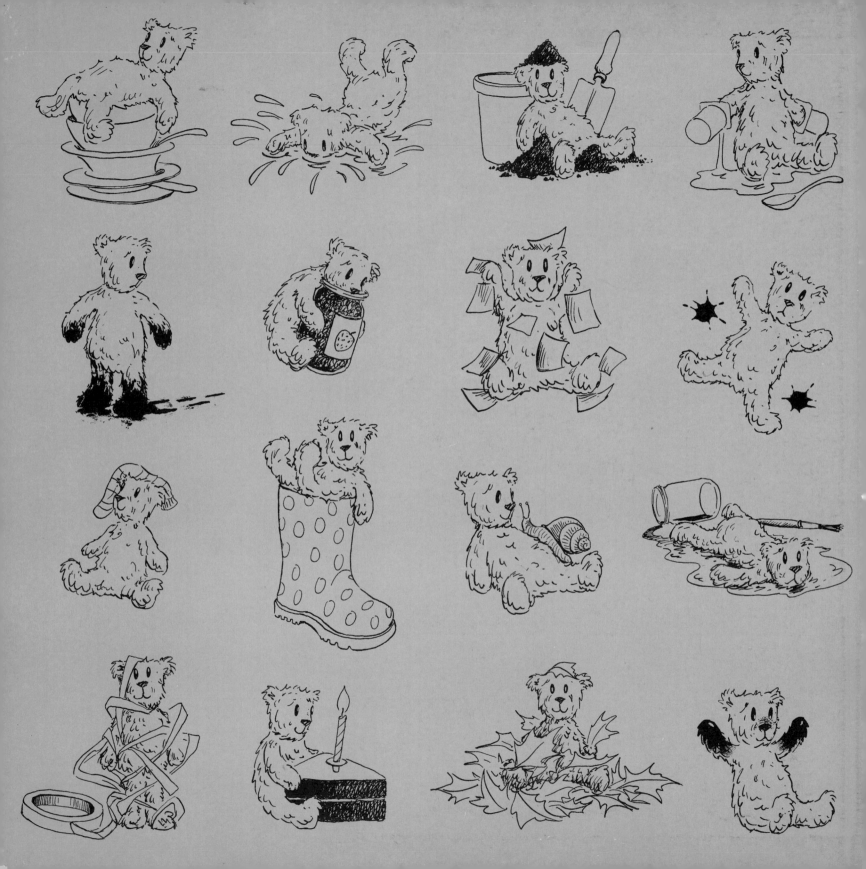